A SWEATER

PIONEER VALLEY EDUCATIONAL PRESS, INC.

Look at the red yarn.

I like red yarn.

3

Look at the purple yarn.

I like purple yarn.

Look at the green yarn.

I like green yarn.

Look at the pink yarn.

I like pink yarn.

Look at the yellow yarn.

I like yellow yarn.

Look at the white yarn.

I like white yarn.

Look at the blue yarn.

I like blue yarn.

Look at me.
I like my sweater.